To Miles—good morning to you.

Library of Congress Cataloging-in-Publication Data available.

ISBN 978-1-4521-7993-3

Manufactured in China.

Design by Abbie Goveia.
Typeset in Capita.
The illustrations in this book were rendered in ink on paper and colored digitally.

10 9 8 7 6 5 4 3 2 1

Chronicle Books LLC
680 Second Street
San Francisco, California 94107

Chronicle Books—we see things differently.
Become part of our community at www.chroniclekids.com.

What Sound Is Morning?

Grant Snider

chronicle books · san francisco

In the first morning light,
all is quiet.

Or is it?

Listen.

What sound is morning?

Lights click on,
a cat softly creeps

a baby babbles,
wind whispers in leaves.

Sprinklers hiss on summer lawns

a rooster crows
to greet the dawn.

The silent sun rises,
the world wakes up

a man shouts after a zooming-off bus.

Cars and trucks grumble
on their way to the city

An old dog yawns,
awake from a dream

frogs croak and splash
in a murmuring stream.

a garbage truck clanks
down a quiet street.

Breakfast sizzles,
hopeful paws tap the floor

in an open field,
balloons rise and roar.

Today is a melody
still to be written,

today is a tune
no one's heard before.

So greet the new day
with a stretch and a yawn

throw open the window

and fill the world
with your song.